Post It!

Facebook Projects for the Real World

Carolyn Bernhardt

Checkerboard Library

An Imprint of Abdo Publishing
abdopublishing.com

abdopublishing.com

Published by Abdo Publishing, a division of ABDO, PO Box 398166, Minneapolis, Minnesota 55439. Copyright © 2017 by Abdo Consulting Group, Inc. International copyrights reserved in all countries. No part of this book may be reproduced in any form without written permission from the publisher. Checkerboard Library™ is a trademark and logo of Abdo Publishing.

Printed in the United States of America, North Mankato, Minnesota

062016
092016

THIS BOOK CONTAINS
RECYCLED MATERIALS

Content Developer: Nancy Tuminelly
Design and Production: Mighty Media, Inc.
Series Editor: Liz Salzmann
Photo Credits: iStockphoto; Mighty Media, Inc.; Shutterstock; Wikimedia Commons

The following manufacturers/names appearing in this book are trademarks: Artist's Loft™, Crayola®, Fiskars®, Office Depot®, Scotch®, Sharpie®

Publishers Cataloging-in-Publication Data
Names: Bernhardt, Carolyn, author.
Title: Post it! : Facebook projects for the real world / by Carolyn Bernhardt.
Description: Minneapolis, MN : Abdo Publishing, [2017] | Series: Cool social media | Includes bibliographical references and index.
Identifiers: LCCN 2016936499 | ISBN 9781680783582 (lib. bdg.) | ISBN 9781680790269 (ebook)
Subjects: LCSH: Facebook (Firm)--Juvenile literature. | Facebook (Electronic resource)--Juvenile literature. | Online social networks--Juvenile literature. | Internet industry--Juvenile literature. | Internet security measures--Juvenile literature.
Classification: DDC 338.4--dc23
LC record available at /http://lccn.loc.gov/2016936499

Contents

What Is
Facebook?

You are spending a week at summer camp. You have photos and videos of your experiences that you want to share. The camp counselor **uploads** this content to the camp's Facebook page. It includes photos of you and your camp friends hiking, a video of the camp talent show, and more! People immediately start liking and commenting on these posts. Now they can share your fun adventure at camp! This is one reason people love Facebook.

Facebook is the most popular social media site in the world. On the site, users can connect and communicate with other users, called "friends," in many ways. Users post **status updates** and upload photos. They can **tag** other users in their posts. They can also comment on and like other users' posts.

Facebookers use the site to stay in touch with friends, plan events, and share important life moments. Facebook has changed the way we communicate. The site makes it easy to connect with **online** communities and share content from around the world!

Facebook
Site Bytes

Purpose: sharing content and connecting with friends

Type of Service: website and app
URL: www.facebook.com
App name: Facebook

Date of Founding: February 4, 2004

Founder: Mark Zuckerberg

Compatible Devices:

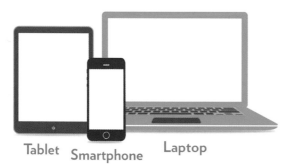

Tablet   Smartphone   Laptop

Tech Terms:

News Feed
A user's News Feed exists on his or her Facebook home page. It shows a constantly updating list of posts from the user's Facebook friends.

Timeline
A Timeline is part of a user's profile. It is a **chronological** list of the user's posts and posts that the user has been **tagged** in.

Founding **Facebook**

Mark Zuckerberg founded Facebook while he was a student at Harvard University in Massachusetts. In 2003, Zuckerberg created a website called Facemash. It was an **online** game using photos of Harvard students. But Zuckerberg didn't have **permission** to use the photos. So, Harvard made Zuckerberg close Facemash.

Soon afterward, Zuckerberg began creating another website. Zuckerberg launched thefacebook on February 4, 2004. It let Harvard students create their own accounts and choose images to **upload**.

Mark Zuckerberg

Thefacebook was instantly popular. Hundreds of students joined in just a few days. In 2005, Zuckerberg changed the website's name to Facebook. In 2006, Facebook became **available** to anyone 13 and older. Today, Facebook has more than 750 million daily users!

Account Info:

- Users must be at least 13 to create an account.

- Once a user creates an account, he or she chooses a username and uploads a profile photo and a cover photo.

- Users find friends on Facebook, searching for them by name and sending them friend requests.

- Users post photos, videos, and **status updates**. And they can like and share their friends' posts.

- Users can also like and follow their favorite organizations and celebrities on Facebook.

- Facebook has privacy **settings** that users can choose from. This allows users to decide what information they share with friends or the public.

Supplies

Here are some of the materials, tools, and devices you'll need to do the projects in this book.

markers

corkboard

adhesive
hook & loop dots

craft foam

clear tape

printer (loaded with paper and ink)

scissors

notebook

pushpins

pin backs

magnetic
tape

Staying Safe

The Internet is a great resource for information. And using it can be a lot of fun! But staying safe **online** is most important. Follow these tips to use social media safely.

* Never try to sign up for a social media account if you are underage. Facebook users must be at least 13 years old.

* Don't share personal information online, especially information people can use to find you in real life. This includes your telephone number and home address.

* Be kind online! Remember that real people post content on the Internet. Do not post rude, hurtful, or mean comments. Report any instances of **cyberbullying** you see to a trusted adult.

* In addition to cyberbullying, report any **inappropriate** content to a trusted adult.

Safety Symbols

Some projects in this book require searching on the Internet. Others require the use of hot tools. That means these projects need some adult help. Determine if you'll need help on a project by looking for these safety symbols.

Hot!
This project requires use of a hot tool.

Internet Use
This project requires searching on the Internet.

Profile Poster from the Past

Create a pretend profile for a famous person from the past!

What you need
- computer
- notebook
- pencil
- printer
- scissors
- poster board
- craft glue
- construction paper
- plain paper
- markers

Frida Kahlo

About
- SURREALIST PAINTER
- BORN IN COYOACÀN, MEXICO
- LIVED IN COYOACÀN, MEXICO
- MARRIED TO DIEGO RIVERA
- BIRTHDAY: JULY 6th, 1907

Timeline
FRIDA KAHLO

I LOVE TO PAINT IN THE SURREALIST STYLE. THIS IS A SELF-PORTRAIT THAT I DID IN 1940.

GUILLERMO KAHLO

I'M SO PROUD OF YOU!

Friends

Many celebrities create Facebook profiles to promote themselves and connect with fans. Imagine that historical figures had Facebook. What types of things would famous inventors, artists, presidents, and other prominent people post? What people and organizations would they like and follow? Choose a historical figure and make a poster of his or her Facebook profile!

1. Think of a historical figure you like or want to learn more about. Have an adult help you research **online** about what the person cared about. What did the person do in his or her lifetime? Check out books from the library. Write down important information about this person in a notebook.

2. Find pictures of your historical figure. Try looking online with adult help. You could also cut images out of magazines and calendars. Choose one photo for the profile picture. Chose another image for the cover photo. Find a few additional pictures you imagine the person would post or be **tagged** in. Print any images you found online. Cut them out.

3. Research your historical figure's family members, peers, and friends. Collect and cut out smaller images of these people.

(continued on the next page)

4. Glue the chosen cover photo to the top of your poster. Glue a strip of construction paper along the bottom of the cover photo.

5. Glue the profile photo over the photo and the construction-paper strip. It should be near the bottom left corner of the cover photo. This resembles the way profile and cover photos appear on Facebook.

6. Write your figure's name on the construction-paper strip.

7. Cut a piece of construction paper big enough to cover the rest of the poster. Glue it in place. This is the background.

8. Cut a rectangle out of plain paper. Make it big enough to cover the right half of the background. Cut three smaller rectangles out of plain paper. They should all fit on the left half of the background. Glue all four rectangles in place.

9. Label the three small rectangles "About," "Friends," and "Likes." Label the large rectangle "Timeline."

10. Write a few important points about your figure in the "About" section. Use information you discovered in your research.

11. Glue the photos of your figure's family members, peers, and friends in the "Friends" section. Add pictures of your figure's favorite things to the "Likes" section.

12. Imagine what your figure and his or her friends might have posted to the Timeline. Add their profile photos to the Timeline. Then write their messages and add other photos.

#funfact
As of December 31, 2015, 1.59 billion people use Facebook each month.

Pet Timeline Tale

Write stories made up
of posts between pets!

What you need

» notebook
» pencil
» computer
» printer
» scissors
» decorative paper
» poster board
» glue stick
» duct tape
» colored paper
» markers

1. What would pets say on Facebook if they had profiles? Pick a favorite pet and find out! Choose a real or made-up pet. Think about what other animal it would connect with on Facebook. What type of **status updates** or photos would your pet post? Write a list of possible Facebook connections. These will be the characters in your story. Create a list of story ideas and topics too. Write a **script** of what the animals would say to one another on Facebook.

2. Choose a profile photo for your pet. It can be your own photo or one you find **online** with adult help. Print several copies of the photo. Cut them out.

3. Repeat step 2 for the other animal characters in your story.

#funfact

Users can set their Facebook accounts to more than 90 languages. One of them is "English (Pirate)"!

(continued on the next page)

4. Choose decorative paper for the poster's background. Cut it to the same size as the poster. You may need to use more than one sheet. Glue it in place. Then put duct tape around the poster's edges for a border.

5. Choose a sheet of colored paper for each pet in your **script**. Cut the sheets into rectangles slightly narrower than the poster. Glue a copy of each pet's profile photo near the top left corner of a rectangle. Write the pet's name above its photo. You should have several rectangles for each pet.

6. Use your script to write posts by the pets. Write each post on a colored rectangle. Make sure you match the posts with the right pets!

7. Glue the posts to the poster. They will resemble a Facebook Timeline. Let the glue dry.

8. Hang up your poster. Add to it as you think of new ideas for your Pet Timeline Tale.

#funfact Buttons

Show what you know with colorful buttons!

What you need

- » computer
- » notebook
- » pencil
- » craft foam
- » objects to trace
- » markers
- » scissors
- » craft glue
- » optional: foam letters, gems, sequins, pom-poms, stickers
- » pin backs
- » hot glue gun & glue sticks

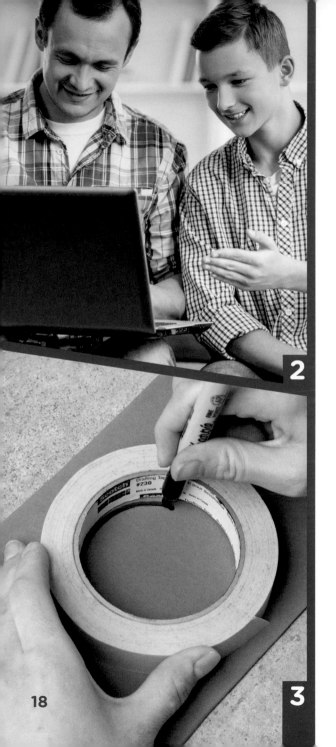

Many companies, organizations, and celebrities post information about their work, products, and lives on Facebook. This is one way they reach their consumers and fans. Visitors can learn a lot by visiting these profiles. Visit the Facebook pages of your favorite magazines, organizations, and celebrities to find fun facts that you can turn into buttons!

1. Have an adult help you visit some kid-friendly public Facebook pages. Search for ones on topics that interest you, or try some of these:

National Geographic Kids: facebook.com/nationalgeographickids

NASA: facebook.com/NASA

Discovery Kids: facebook.com/DiscoveryKids

Nickelodeon: facebook.com/nickelodeon

Disney: facebook.com/Disney

2. Scroll through the Facebook pages and read the posts. Click on and read articles. Watch videos. Search for fun facts. Write down your favorite facts in a notebook.

3. Decide what shapes you want your buttons to be. Find objects in those shapes to trace onto craft foam. Cut out the shapes.

4. Turn the shapes over so the marker lines are on the bottom. Write a fun fact on each one. Use markers or foam letters. Don't forget to include the **hashtag** #funfact!

5. Decorate the buttons. Cut small shapes out of craft foam. Glue them to the buttons. Add gems, stickers, or small drawings. Get creative!

6. Hot glue a pin back to the back of each button. Let the glue dry.

7. Attach your buttons to your backpack or favorite jacket. Or, wear a different #funfact button each day!

Real-Life Like Button

Give a few of your favorite things
a big thumbs-up!

Each Facebook post has a Like button. Users can click it to show that they like the post. When a user likes something, that content appears in the timelines of the user's friends and followers. Create a giant magnet that resembles Facebook's Like button to show people what you like most!

1. On craft foam, draw an outline of a hand giving the thumbs-up sign. Include the wrist and sleeve cuff.

2. Trace the pencil lines with a marker. Cut out the hand and wrist.

3. Decorate the sleeve cuff. Glue another color of craft foam over it or color it with markers. Add stripes or buttons. Get creative!

4. Stick a strip of magnetic tape to the back of the hand.

5. Use your Like button to hang favorite photos, notes, or quotes on your refrigerator. Make more magnetic Like buttons to hang even more items!

Connection Map

String together your connections to
visualize your web of friends and family!

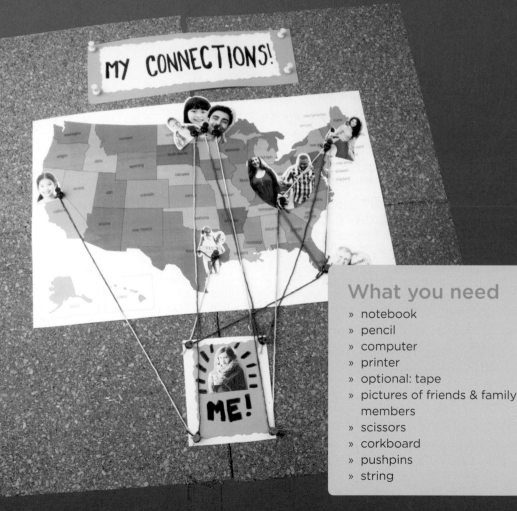

What you need

» notebook
» pencil
» computer
» printer
» optional: tape
» pictures of friends & family
  members
» scissors
» corkboard
» pushpins
» string

Facebook allows friends and family members from all over the world to connect **online**. Users' profiles list the other Facebookers they are friends with. This list also shows which friends users have in common. These are labeled "Mutual Friends." Create a physical map of your mutual friends within your city or state, or around the world!

1. Make a list of people you know. This could include friends, family members, classmates, teachers, and pen pals. List the cities, states, or countries these people live in. Look at your list of locations. Decide if you will need a world map, country map, or state map.

2. Have an adult help you find a map online. Print the map as large as possible. You may need to print parts of it on different sheets of paper. These can be taped together to create the whole map.

3. Gather pictures of the people on your list. Find one of yourself too. Trim the images to whatever size you like.

(continued on the next page)

4. Attach the map to corkboard with pushpins.

5. Pin the photos of your connections to the locations where they live.

6. Pin the photo of yourself near the map.

7. Cut a long piece of string for each of your connections. Tie one end of each string to a pin holding the photo of yourself.

#funfact
More than 80 percent of Facebook users live outside the United States and Canada.

8. Wrap each string around a pin holding the photo of a connection. Leave the ends of the strings hanging loose.

9. Think about how your friends are connected other than through you. Your relatives probably know one another. So do your classmates. Use the hanging strings to connect people who know each other. For example, you and your cousin have the same grandfather. Your cousin lives in New York. Your grandfather lives in Cuba. Both your cousin and grandfather should have strings connecting to your photo and a string connecting the two of them.

10. Continue using string to connect everyone you know. Cut more string as you need it.

11. Stand back and admire your map. Are many of your friends and family members connected? Were you surprised to discover any new connections?

12. Add to your map as you make new friends and meet new people!

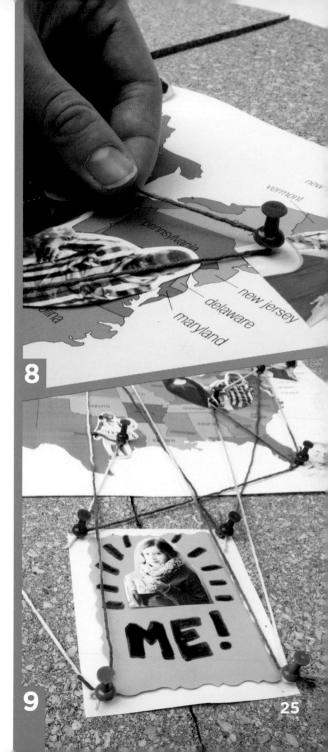

Easy Emoticon Frame

Make mini reaction magnets for your favorite framed photo!

What you need
» framed photo
» permanent markers
» computer
» craft foam
» coins
» scissors
» adhesive hook & loop dots

1. Select a framed photo to use. Ask for **permission** to use the photo. Use a marker to write "Reaction" on the top of the frame.

2. Facebook has six reaction buttons. They represent "like," "love," "ha ha," "wow," "sad," and "angry." Have an adult help you research these buttons **online**. You will create buttons that look similar. You can also make up your own **emoticons**.

3. Trace a coin six times on craft foam to create a round base for each emoticon. Use a different color for each one.

4. Decorate your emoticon buttons to show the different reactions. Cut them out.

5. Stick a fuzzy hook & loop dot to the back of each button. Stick six scratchy hook & loop dots along the bottom of the frame. Stick one scratchy hook & loop dot next to the word "Reaction."

6. Display your framed photo. As friends and family members view it, they can choose a reaction to place at the top of the frame.

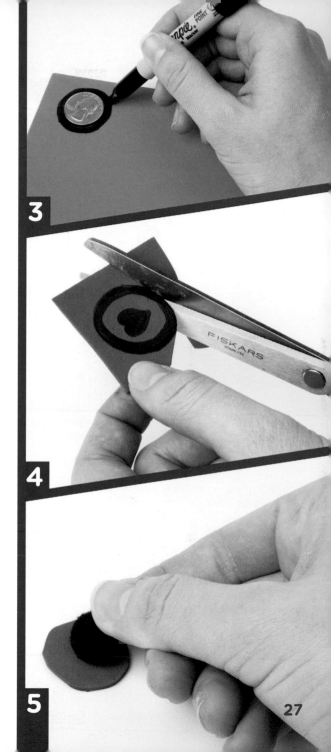

27

Reaction Lab

Invent new emoticons to communicate different reactions!

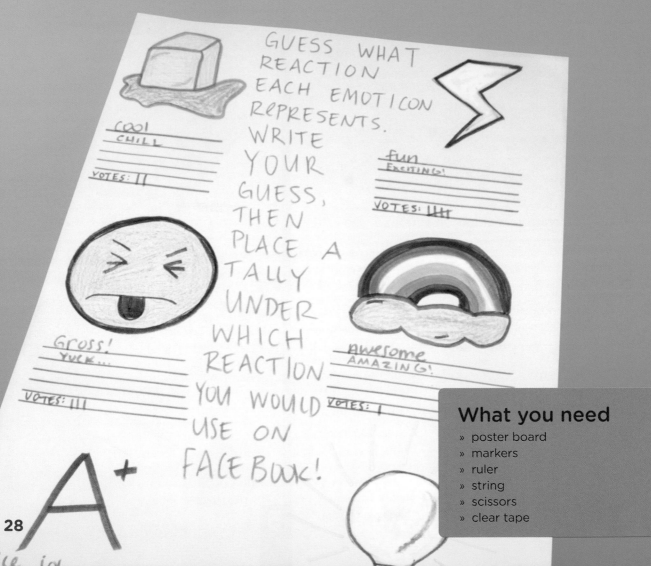

GUESS WHAT REACTION EACH EMOTICON REPRESENTS. WRITE YOUR GUESS, THEN PLACE A TALLY UNDER WHICH REACTION YOU WOULD USE ON FACEBOOK!

COOL
CHILL
VOTES: II

FUN
EXCITING!
VOTES: IIII

Gross!
YUCK...
VOTES: III

awesome
AMAZING!
VOTES: I

A+
Nice in

What you need
» poster board
» markers
» ruler
» string
» scissors
» clear tape

28

On February 24, 2016, Facebook added reaction buttons. These six **emoticons** represent serious, silly, or fun reactions to Facebook content. This allows users to express more than they could with just the Like button. Create your own reaction buttons! Have your friends and family members guess the reaction behind each button. They can then vote for their favorite.

1. Think of six reactions. These could include happiness, sadness, anger, excitement, laughter, or love. Try to think of reactions that would be easy to represent as emoticons. For example, the reaction "gross!" might be an emoticon of a face sticking its tongue out. A reaction of "cool" might be an ice cube.

2. Draw your six emoticons on the poster board. Get creative as you draw and decorate them.

3. Use the ruler to draw five to six lines under each emoticon. Write "Votes" on the last line under each emoticon.

(continued on the next page)

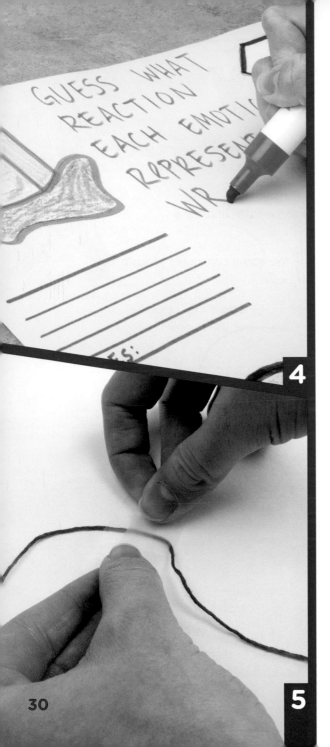

4. Write the instructions on the poster. They should say, "Guess what reaction each **emoticon** represents. Write your guess, then place a **tally** under which reaction you would use on Facebook!"

5. Cut a long piece of string and tie one end to a marker. Tape the other end to the back of the poster.

6. Hang your poster at home or at school. Make sure you get **permission** first. Have people guess the reactions and vote for their favorites. Which reaction button was the most popular? Do you think users would like to have this reaction button on Facebook?

#funfact

In October 2015, soccer star Cristiano Ronaldo became the first athlete to get 100 million likes on Facebook.

Glossary

available – able to be had or used.

chronological – arranged in or according to the order of time.

cyberbully – to tease, hurt, or threaten someone online.

emoticon – a small image used in e-mail and apps to communicate a feeling or attitude.

hashtag – a label often included in online posts that includes the symbol # followed by a word or phrase.

inappropriate – not suitable, fitting, or proper.

online – connected to the Internet.

permission – 1. formal consent. 2. when a person in charge says it's okay to do something.

script – the written text for a performance.

setting – the way a computer program is set or adjusted.

status update – a post on social media that describes what the user is doing or feeling.

tag – to add a name or location to an online post.

tally – a mark used to keep count of something.

upload – to transfer data from a computer to a larger network.

Websites

To learn more about Cool Social Media, visit **booklinks.abdopublishing.com**. These links are routinely monitored and updated to provide the most current information available.

Index